CUMBRIA LIBRARIES

3 8003 04825 1557

KT-151-644

Welcome to Percy's Park!

Percy the park keeper
works hard looking after
the park and his animal
friends who live there.
But Percy still likes to
find time for some fun
and games. And, of
course, in Percy's Park,
there's always time
for a story…

Percy's Bumpy Ride

First published in hardback in Great Britain by HarperCollins Publishers Ltd in 1999
First published in paperback by Picture Lions in 2000
New edition published by Collins Picture Books in 2003
This edition published by HarperCollins Children's Books in 2011

15

ISBN: 978-0-00-715514-9

Picture Lions and Collins Picture Books are imprints of the Children's Division,
part of HarperCollins Publishers Ltd.
HarperCollins Children's Books is a division of HarperCollins Publishers Ltd.

Text and illustrations copyright © Nick Butterworth 1999, 2011

The author/illustrator asserts the moral right to be identified
as the author/illustrator of the work.

A CIP catalogue record for this title is available from the British Library. All rights reserved.
No part of this publication may be reproduced, stored in a retrieval system or transmitted in any
form or by any means, electronic, mechanical, photocopying, recording or otherwise, without the
prior permission of HarperCollins Publishers Ltd, 1 London Bridge Street, London SE1 9GF.

Visit our website at: www.harpercollins.co.uk

Printed in China

Nick Butterworth

Percy's Bumpy Ride

HarperCollins *Children's Books*

Percy the park keeper was hard at work. Bang! Bang! Bang! Bang! Squeak, squeak, squeak. Tap, tap, tappity-tap. Bang! Bang! Ouch!

For three whole days, sounds like these had been coming from Percy's workshop. What was he doing? Percy's friends, the animals who lived in the park, could only guess.

"I think he's making a bird table," said a squirrel.

"It could be a park bench," said a rabbit.

"It might be a…" But nobody heard what the hedgehog thought it might be.

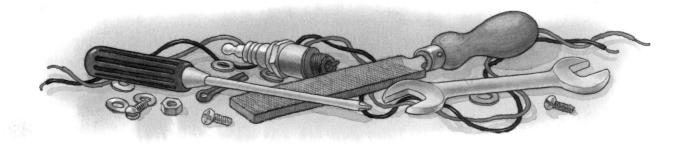

At that moment, there came the roar of an engine. The workshop doors burst open and above the noise of the engine, they heard Percy's voice.

"Make way! Make way!"

With a great clanking sound and a lot of smoke, Percy emerged from the workshop sitting on top of a very strange machine.

Percy pushed a switch and the engine coughed and spluttered into silence.

"Well," said Percy, "what do you think?"

"I know what I think," said the fox.

"I think, *what is it?*"

"This is my new lawn mower," said Percy, patting the machine. "I've got terribly behind with cutting the grass. My old mower is so slow. But with this, I'll just fly around the park."

"Will it really fly?" asked a hedgehog.

"It's a lawn mower," chuckled Percy. "The propeller on top is to fan me with cool air while I'm mowing."

Percy turned a key and the engine clanked into life again.

"Come on," he said. "Let's try it out. All aboard!"

With everyone sitting on his new mower, Percy began to chug across the grass.

"It works!" shouted Percy as he admired the stripe of closely cut grass behind the mower. "Let's try it a bit faster."

Percy pushed a lever. But what happened next
took everyone by surprise.

The engine roared and the propeller whirled faster and faster. Then, to everyone's astonishment, Percy's mower began to lift into the air.

"It does fly!" squealed the hedgehog. "You're so clever, Percy!"

"Er, well, I wouldn't say that," said Percy as he struggled with the mower's controls. He was beginning to think that the propeller was not such a good idea.

At first, the flying mower
seemed to be deciding
all by itself where to go.
But after a while, Percy found that by
pushing and pulling levers he could make
the mower go where he wanted.

For the animals it was very
exciting. Only the ducks and the
owl had ever been this high
up in the air before.

Suddenly the badger
called out.

"Tree ahead, Percy!"

"Oh, er, thank you,"
said Percy.

He pulled hard on a
lever and just managed
to swoop over the
tall tree, mowing
some leaves as
he passed.

As the mower climbed high into the sky, the animals were amazed by what they could see below them.

"Look at those sheep," said one of the rabbits. "They've made a shape like a hand. I think they're waving to us."

"I doubt it," said Percy. "I shouldn't think they've even noticed us."

"I think they have noticed us," said the rabbit. "Look!"

The sheep had now arranged themselves into the shape of a face.

It looked very much like a face they all knew.

Everyone waved to the sheep.

Percy wished he could join them.

He didn't realise how quickly his wish would be granted.

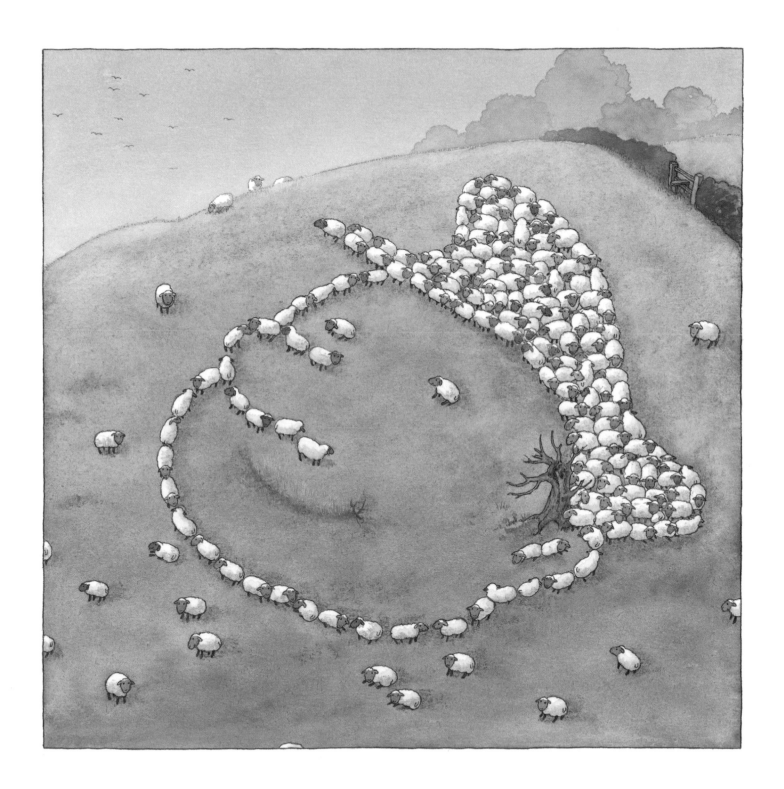

Whether the spinning propeller on top of
the mower had begun to feel giddy, or
whether it had just had enough of turning round
and round, no one could be sure. But suddenly,
it stopped. And just as suddenly, so did the
mower's engine.

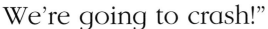

"That's better," said the fox. "It's nice and quiet."
"It's quiet," said Percy, "but it's not nice.
We're going to crash!"

Down went the mower and down went the
mower's passengers.

"It's such a pity you don't have wings," said the owl.
"Isn't it!" said Percy, as he shot past her.

The sheep below looked worried.
They began to run all over the field.

"Get out of the way!" shouted Percy.

But the sheep didn't. Instead, they huddled together, right under where Percy and the animals were falling.

Then Percy realised what the sheep were doing.

Now, instead of the hard ground below him, Percy looked down to see a soft, springy, woolly blanket.

The badger was the first to land. As each one landed, they bounced on the soft, woolly backs of the sheep.

Even Percy, the heaviest of all, bounced
three times and was safely down.

Everyone said a big thank you to the sheep. They laughed and said they were very glad to help. They were only sorry they couldn't save Percy's mower.

Percy looked to where the mower had crash-landed in a tree.

"I won't be using that again," he said.

"What will you do?" said the hedgehog. "The grass in the park is still very long."

Percy sighed and scratched his head. Then he began to smile.

"Er…sheep," said Percy. "How would you like to visit a field of lovely, long, tasty, green grass..?"

"I was born in London in 1946 and grew up in a sweet shop in Essex. For several years I worked as a graphic designer, but in 1980 I decided to concentrate on writing and illustrating books for children.

My wife, Annette, and I have two grown-up children, Ben and Amanda, and we have put down roots in the country.

I haven't recently counted how many books there are with my name on the cover but Percy the Park Keeper accounts for a good many of them. I'm reliably informed that they have sold in their millions, worldwide. Hooray!

I didn't realise this when I invented Percy, but I can now see that he's very like my mum's dad, my grandpa. Here's a picture of him giving a ride to my mum and my brother, Mike, in his old home-made wheelbarrow!"

Nick Butterworth

Nick Butterworth has presented children's stories on television, worked on a strip for *Sunday Express Magazine* and worked for various major graphic design companies. Among his books published by HarperCollins are *Thud!*, *QPootle5*, *Jingle Bells*, *Albert le Blanc*, *Tiger* and *The Whisperer*, which won the Nestlé Gold Award. But he is best known for his stories about Percy the Park Keeper. There are now more than 30 books about Percy, who features on audio CD and DVD, as well as having appeared in his own television series.

Collect all the Percy the Park Keeper stories
OVER 7 MILLION BOOKS SOLD!

PB: 978-0-00-714693-2

PB: 978-0-00-715515-6

PB: 978-0-00-715516-3

PB: 978-0-00-715518-7

PB: 978-0-00-715517-0

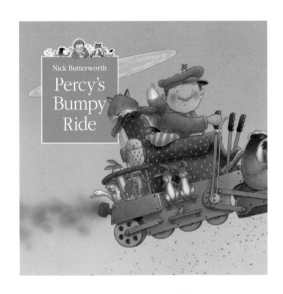

PB: 978-0-00-715514-9

Percy the Park Keeper stories can be ordered at:

www.harpercollins.co.uk